FC DALLAS

BY SAM MOUSSAVI

SportsZone

An Imprint of Abdo Publishing
abdobooks.com

abdobooks.com

Published by Abdo Publishing, a division of ABDO, PO Box 398166, Minneapolis, Minnesota 55439. Copyright © 2022 by Abdo Consulting Group, Inc. International copyrights reserved in all countries. No part of this book may be reproduced in any form without written permission from the publisher. SportsZone™ is a trademark and logo of Abdo Publishing.

Printed in the United States of America, North Mankato, Minnesota
052021
092021

Cover Photo: Matt Ferris/Image of Sport/AP Images
Interior Photos: Brad Loper/AP Images, 4–5; Chuck Myers/Cal Sport Media/AP Images, 6; Andrew Dieb/Icon Sportswire/AP Images, 8; Mo Khursheed/TFV Media/AP Images, 10–11; Jeffery McWhorter/AP Images, 13; John G. Zimmerman/Sports Illustrated/Set Number: X17936 TK2 R4 F22/Getty Images, 15; Ronald Martinez/Allsport/Getty Images Sport/Getty Images, 17; Chris Putnam/AP Images, 18; Stephan Savoia/AP Images, 21; Gus Ruelas/AP Images, 22; Andy Lyons/AllsportGetty Images Sport/Getty Images, 25; Bill Kostroun/AP Images, 26, 28; Mark J. Terrill/AP Images, 31; Matthew Visinsky/Icon Sportswire/AP Images, 32, 42; Stephen Dunn/Getty Images Sport/Getty Images, 34–35; Simon Bruty/Allsport/Getty Images Sport/Getty Images, 36; Wayne Gooden/Image of Sport/AP Images, 39; LM Otero/AP Images, 41

Editor: Patrick Donnelly
Series Designer: Dan Peluso

Library of Congress Control Number: 2019954374

Publisher's Cataloging-in-Publication Data

Names: Moussavi, Sam, author.
Title: FC Dallas / by Sam Moussavi
Description: Minneapolis, Minnesota : Abdo Publishing, 2022 | Series: Inside MLS | Includes online resources and index.
Identifiers: ISBN 9781532192562 (lib. bdg.) | ISBN 9781098210465 (ebook)
Subjects: LCSH: FC Dallas (Soccer team)--Juvenile literature. | Soccer teams--Juvenile literature. | Professional sports franchises--Juvenile literature. | Sports Teams--Juvenile literature.
Classification: DDC 796.334--dc23

TABLE OF CONTENTS

CHAPTER 1

CHASING
THE SHIELD

FC Dallas fans had little to complain about in 2015. The Major League Soccer (MLS) team won 18 games in the regular season, one shy of the franchise record. Those 18 wins plus six draws added up to 60 points. That was also a record for FC Dallas. No other MLS club earned more points that year.

But the Toros—as FC Dallas is commonly called—were matched atop the standings by the New York Red Bulls. And New York's goal differential of plus-19 topped the Toros' plus-13 differential. That meant the Red Bulls won the MLS Supporters' Shield. That trophy is given each year to the team with the best regular-season record.

Still, the Toros hoped to make their mark in the playoffs. With New York in the Eastern Conference, Dallas held the

FC Dallas players celebrate a playoff victory over Seattle in 2015.

Michael Barrios, *center*, celebrates one of his goals against DC United as Aaron Guillen, *left*, and Maxi Urruti look on.

top seed in the West. The Toros met the fourth-seeded Seattle Sounders in the conference semifinals. Each team would host one game. And each won its home game 2–1. That meant a penalty kick shootout would decide which team advanced. When 22-year-old defender Walker Zimmerman converted his chance, the Toros had the victory.

The Toros lost to the Portland Timbers by an aggregate score of 5–3 in the Western Conference finals. But the 2015 season was one of the most successful in team history. With that foundation in place, the team had high hopes going into the 2016 season.

STARTING STRONG

Dallas fielded one of the deepest rosters in team history that year. The Toros played especially well early in the season. They won three out of their first four matches, outscoring opponents 7–0 in the victories. Argentine striker Maxi Urruti scored three of those goals. Colombian winger Michael Barrios scored twice in a 3–0 win at DC United. That victory was a statement to the rest of the league. The Toros matched up well with some of the better teams in MLS.

After three straight road losses, FC Dallas went on a tear starting in mid-May. They posted six wins and two draws in their next nine matches. And while the team's offense was inconsistent, the Toros played tough defense all season. Defender Matt Hedges and goalkeeper Chris Seitz were the backbone of the league's fourth-best defense. FC Dallas gave up an average of only 1.2 goals per match in 2016.

Toros forward Mauro Rosales races down the field against the Chicago Fire in 2016.

Eleven of the team's final 13 regular-season matches resulted in either wins or draws. One of those wins came on July 16 against the Chicago Fire. The teams have been rivals since 1998, when Chicago joined MLS and FC Dallas went by its original name, the Dallas Burn. Each season the two teams play for the right to raise the Brimstone Cup.

The Brimstone Cup was originally given its name because both teams had names connected to fire. The trophy is awarded to the team that earns the most points in the rivalry games each season. The teams' supporters' groups created the Brimstone Cup in 2001. It was the league's first rivalry trophy. The traveling trophy stays with the winner until the next season's Brimstone Cup is played.

The Toros' offense put on a show in front of its home crowd in the 2016 Brimstone Cup. Urruti once again led the charge with an early goal, and Dallas never looked back. Behind two more goals and a stingy defense, Dallas defeated Chicago 3–1. With the win, the Toros brought home the Brimstone Cup for the first time in five seasons.

US OPEN CUP CHAMPS

The US Open Cup is a knockout tournament that is open to teams across the country, from MLS down to amateur leagues. In 2016 FC Dallas won four matches in a row to make it to the US Open Cup final for the fourth time in team history. In the final the Toros defeated the New England Revolution 4–2. Coupled with their Supporters' Shield win, that made 2016 doubly successful in Dallas.

The Toros celebrate their 2016 US Open Cup championship after defeating the New England Revolution in the final.

FC Dallas finished the regular season with 17 wins, just shy of its 2015 mark. The Toros also earned 60 points for the second straight season. That was good enough for first place in the Western Conference. The Red Bulls once again won the Eastern

Conference title. But this time they finished with 57 points, meaning FC Dallas picked up its first Supporters' Shield.

Urruti and Barrios tied for the team lead in goals with nine. Argentine midfielder Mauro Díaz, masterful at setting up his teammates, had 10 assists during the regular season. Díaz also added five goals for good measure. In total 13 players scored for FC Dallas in 2016, a sign of the roster's depth. Now the question was whether that depth would have the same impact in the playoffs.

FRUSTRATING FINISH

After receiving a bye in the first round, FC Dallas faced the Seattle Sounders in the Western Conference semifinals. It would be a two-match series decided on aggregate. The Toros had won two of their three regular-season matches. But the one loss came by a score of 5–0 at Seattle. That outcome proved to be ominous when the Sounders cruised to a 3–0 home victory in the first game of the series.

That meant the Toros would have to win the second match back in Dallas by more than three goals. The pressure was on. That desperation from Dallas opened up a scoring chance for Seattle in the 16th minute, but the Sounders' shot missed the goal.

Dallas got on the board in the 25th minute on a goal by Tesho Akindele. Shortly after halftime Seattle tied it up. Two minutes later Urruti put the Toros back on top 2–1. But that was all the offense Dallas could muster. The Toros won the match

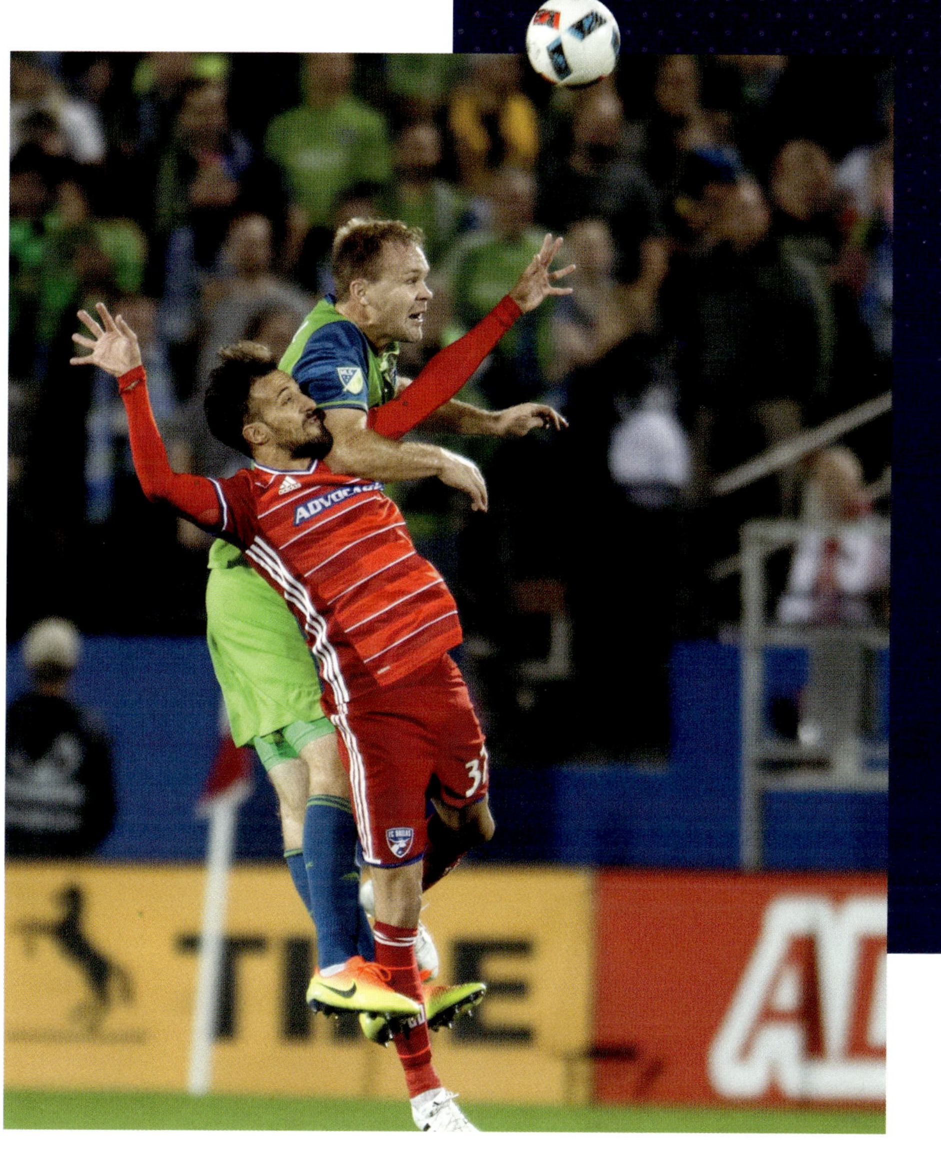

Chad Marshall, *top*, beats Urruti to a header in the Toros' playoff defeat at Seattle in 2016.

2–1 but lost on aggregate 4–2. It was a bittersweet end to a memorable season for the Toros. But not all was lost. FC Dallas had added some valuable hardware to its trophy case that year.

CHAPTER 2

FROM
BURN TO FC

Texas is known as football country—as in American football. However, the Lone Star State has also had a rich soccer history. The Dallas Tornado were one of the first professional soccer teams in America. The Tornado formed in 1967 and played in the North American Soccer League (NASL) from 1968 to 1981. The team won an NASL title in 1971 and had many prominent players, including Kyle Rote Jr., the only US-born player ever to lead the NASL in scoring.

Those Tornado teams left an important legacy, too. They imported European talent to play with their homegrown American players. In addition to playing, many of those European players coached soccer clinics in the Dallas area.

Kyle Rote Jr., one of the early stars of the NASL, makes a diving header for the Tornado in 1973.

The clinics helped create interest in soccer as well as develop young talent in the area.

After the United States hosted the 1994 World Cup, the popularity of soccer was at an all-time high in North America. The city of Dallas was awarded an MLS franchise in the summer of 1995. Kansas City and Colorado also were announced as MLS cities on the same day as Dallas. The teams would begin play in 1996 as three of the league's 10 charter members.

BIRTH OF THE BURN

The team was originally named the Dallas Burn. The name was tied to two state symbols: the oilfields and the hot Texas sun. Dallas would play its home games at the Cotton Bowl. That stadium was famous for hosting a major college football bowl game each year.

The Burn played their first game on April 14, 1996, hosting the San Jose Clash. Neither team was able to score in regulation. However, the Burn won by shootout in front of 27,779 fans. Four days later, Dallas hosted the Kansas City Wiz. Midfielder Jason Kreis scored the franchise's first goal as the home team won 3–0.

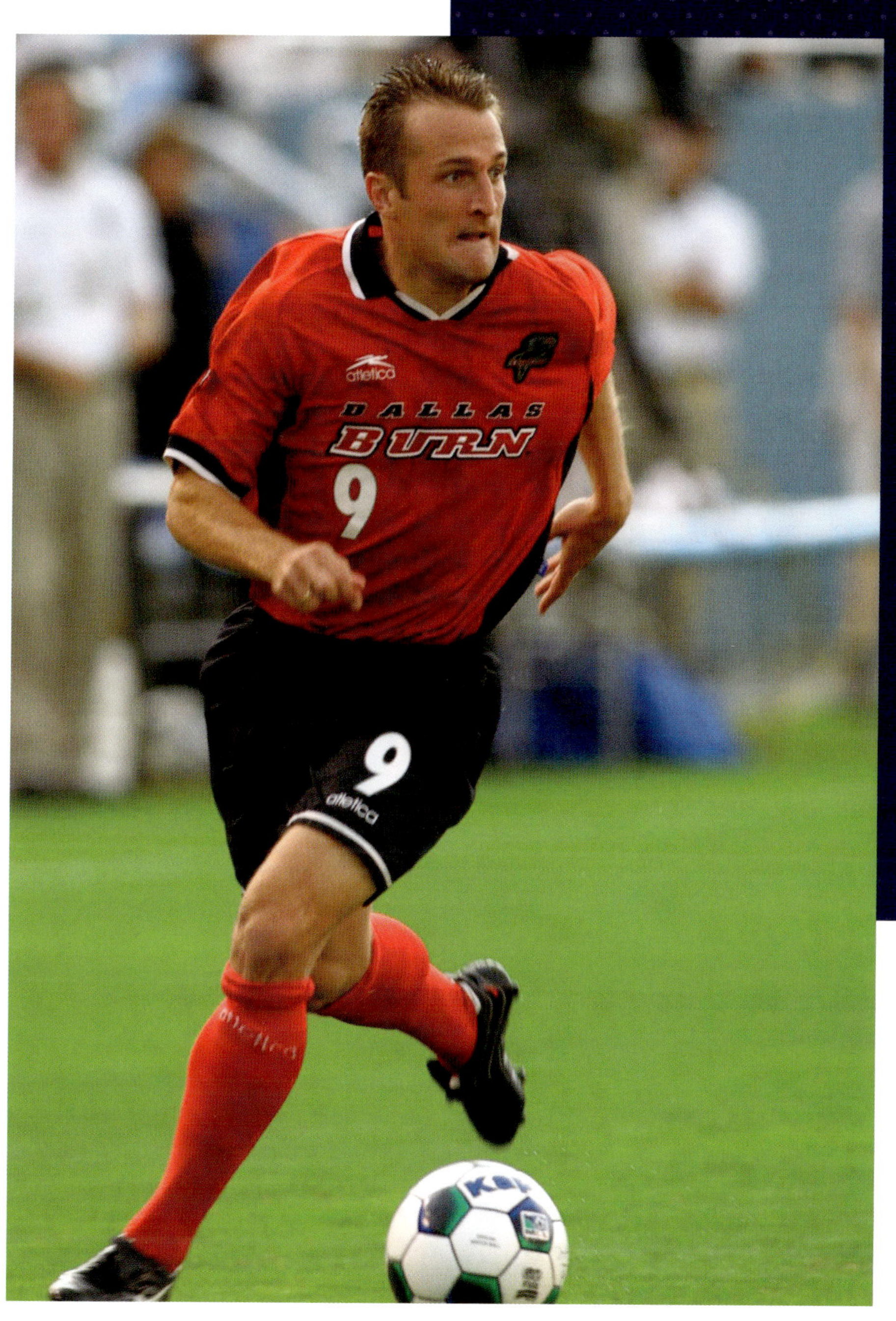

Jason Kreis was one of the Burn's early stars.

Óscar Pareja of the Burn and Manny Lagos of the Columbus Crew fight for the ball in a 2004 match.

Kreis went on to score 13 goals that season, tied for seventh in the league. Dallas finished the season in second place in the Western Conference. However, the team lost its first playoff series, a best-of-three matchup against Kansas City.

Though Dallas fell short of the MLS Cup, it was a solid start for the Burn. High-scoring forwards Dante Washington and Damián Álvarez led them back to the playoffs the next year. This time Dallas won its first playoff series against the LA Galaxy before losing to Colorado in the conference finals. But two weeks after their defeat in the MLS playoffs, the Burn made history by winning their first trophy. In the US Open Cup final, Dallas defeated original MLS powerhouse DC United in a shootout after a scoreless 120 minutes.

The progress continued for the Burn. In 1999 they had their finest season to date, earning 57 points during the regular season. That was good for second place in the West. In the playoffs Dallas made it to the Western Conference finals before falling to the Galaxy. Kreis earned

DODD SHUTS THE DOOR

Goalkeeper Mark Dodd was born in Dallas and was the Burn's first keeper in 1996. Dodd started 31 games in the Burn's first season and won the MLS Goalkeeper of the Year Award. In total he made 92 appearances during his four seasons with the Burn.

the MLS Most Valuable Player (MVP) Award after tying for the league lead with 18 goals. And the defense surrendered just 35 goals in 32 games, second-fewest in MLS.

The Burn made the playoffs in their first seven MLS seasons. But they became known for their inability to win the big one. Without an MLS Cup win, Dallas struggled to make a mark in a part of the country where football is king. Team ownership decided to shake things up.

BURN OUT

The team changed its name from Dallas Burn to FC Dallas prior to the 2005 season. The new identity was intended to be more in line with soccer traditions. A new team crest featured a Texas longhorn, while the team adopted red, white, and blue colors that matched both the US and Texas flags.

That wasn't the only change. Like many early MLS teams, the team had been playing in a stadium much larger than it needed to be. All the empty seats took away from the atmosphere at the Cotton Bowl. So the team also built a new stadium and training facility in the nearby city of Frisco, Texas. With 21,000 seats, the stadium was better suited for soccer crowds. And the stadium was designed specifically for soccer. In fact, FC Dallas's new stadium would be only the third

FC Dallas midfielder Simo Valakari (17) makes a sliding tackle against New England Revolution midfielder Jose Cancela during a 2005 match.

soccer-specific stadium in MLS. The team played its first home game at what was then called Pizza Hut Park on August 6, 2005.

FC Dallas players celebrate their upset of the LA Galaxy in the 2010 Western Conference final.

With a new identity and a new place to call home, FC Dallas returned to consistent winning. It finished in the top five in the league the next three seasons. But again the club could not make it past the Western Conference semifinals.

That changed in 2010. FC Dallas finished third in the conference. Midfielder David Ferreira won the MLS MVP Award that year after posting eight goals and 13 assists. However, few expected much of a playoff run for the Toros. The team was a heavy underdog against Real Salt Lake, that year's runner-up for the Supporters' Shield. But Dallas proved to be up for the challenge, upsetting RSL on aggregate.

Next up for the Toros was an old rival, the LA Galaxy. International superstars David Beckham and Landon Donovan had carried the Galaxy to the best record in the league. But once again Dallas did the unthinkable. The Toros shocked LA 3–0 on the road to reach their first MLS Cup. However, an own goal in extra time provided a heartbreaking end to the season as the Toros fell to the Colorado Rapids 2–1.

The Toros had their ups and downs the rest of the decade, peaking with their Supporters' Shield and US Open Cup victories in 2016. But their inability to get over their struggles in the MLS playoffs continued to haunt them.

CHAPTER 3

TEXAS-SIZED TOROS

The story of FC Dallas cannot be told without a discussion of two important coaches. Dave Dir became the first MLS employee when he was hired in 1993. Among his duties was helping put together the group of players who would be divided among the league's original 10 teams. That experience gave him unique insight into the league's talent. And so in 1995 the Dallas Burn hired him to be their first head coach.

Dir coached the Burn from 1996 to 2000. By the end of his run in Dallas his teams had won 81 regular-season games. At the time this was more than any other head coach in MLS history. He also guided the Burn to the US Open Cup title in 1997.

Dave Dir gives directions to his players in a 2000 game.

Carlos Ruíz holds off New York Red Bulls defender Jeff Parke in a rainy 2007 match.

Dir was Dallas' most notable head coach until Óscar Pareja arrived. Born in Colombia, Pareja played professional soccer for 18 years, eight of them with Dallas. His professional playing career ended in 2005. Pareja then decided to get into coaching.

Pareja initially spent two seasons as an assistant coach with FC Dallas starting in 2006. He then left the club to pursue other coaching opportunities. On January 10, 2014, Pareja was named the sixth head coach of FC Dallas. He held the position until the end of the 2018 season.

In five seasons, Pareja's FC Dallas teams won 97 games. That gave him the most coaching wins in team history. Pareja led the team to the Supporters' Shield and a US Open Cup title in 2016.

HIGH-SCORING HEROES

Jason Kreis was drafted 43rd overall by the Burn in the first MLS Draft in 1996. He made a big impact in his rookie season, scoring the first goal in Dallas Burn history. The midfielder scored 91 goals in his Dallas career, the most in franchise history.

Kreis was a consistent contributor through his nine seasons in Dallas. He led his team in goals five times. In 1999 he was

Kenny Cooper (33) and Ruíz celebrate a goal in 2006.

the first US-born player to be named league MVP. During that season, Kreis led the league in points and goals. He also registered the first 15-goal, 15-assist season in league history. The five-time MLS all-star left FC Dallas after the 2004 season.

After Kreis left, FC Dallas needed some star power to fill in the gap. Carlos Ruíz fit that description. The native of Guatemala had won the 2002 MLS MVP Award. He'd also established himself as one of the league's best scorers during three seasons with the LA Galaxy. The player nicknamed *El Pescadito*, Spanish for "Little Fish," kept that up after being traded to Dallas in 2005.

The striker finished the 2005 season with a team-leading 11 goals. The next year Ruíz upped that total to 13, still more than any other Toro. His most memorable goal with the Toros came on a bicycle kick against DC United in 2005. That play was selected as the MLS Goal of the Decade.

Ruíz left FC Dallas in 2007, only to return to the club for one final match in 2016. He scored in that one, too. By the end of his second stint in the Lone Star State, he had scored 37 goals for Dallas. That mark is good for third place in franchise history. His 16 postseason goals make him the leader for the most playoff goals in MLS history.

FAMILIAR NAME

Forward Kenny Cooper would help pick up some of the slack after Ruíz left. But first they had a brief but successful run together. Cooper's father, Kenny Sr., was a former English goalkeeper who spent 10 years in Dallas playing for the NASL's Tornado. Kenny Jr. joined FC Dallas in 2006 and made an immediate impact. He finished his first FC Dallas campaign with 11 goals, second only to Ruíz.

At the start of the 2007 season, Cooper scored four goals in the first eight games. But he broke a bone in his right leg in a match against the LA Galaxy. The injury put him out for a majority of the season. The team struggled without him. But Cooper returned the next year and put together a career year.

Cooper led FC Dallas with 18 goals in 30 starts in 2008. He was the club's only player to appear in every regular-season game. Cooper finished the season tied for the league lead with four game-winning goals. He won the MLS Comeback Player of the Year Award.

Forward Jeff Cunningham came to FC Dallas in a trade with Toronto FC in 2008. Cunningham scored in his first match as an FC Dallas player on August 16, 2008. The goal was his 100th in

Jeff Cunningham, *left*, beats LA Galaxy keeper Donovan Ricketts for a goal in 2009.

his MLS career. Cunningham scored five goals in 11 games with the Toros that year.

In 2009 Cunningham emerged as the team's go-to scorer. He scored four goals in one game against the Kansas City Wizards. After burying seven goals in five games in September, Cunningham won MLS Player of the Month. He went on to win the 2009 MLS Golden Boot, having scored 17 times in 28 games.

Jesús Ferreira is one of the more promising young talents in MLS.

Cunningham left FC Dallas after the 2010 season to play one final MLS season with the Columbus Crew. He scored 33 goals during his time with the Toros. His 134 career regular-season goals put him in second place on the all-time MLS goals list.

New stars emerged in the years that followed. Veteran midfielder Michael Barrios played six seasons in Dallas from 2015 to 2020. During that time the quick-footed Colombia native scored 31 goals and added 44 assists. No MLS player had more than his 13 assists in 2019.

Many of those assists went to forward Jesús Ferreira. The son of former FC Dallas superstar David Ferreira, he scored eight goals in 2019 at just 18 years old. Once again FC Dallas showed that it was a place where young players could thrive.

HOMEGROWN TOROS

Many MLS teams have tried to improve their roster by importing foreign players. But FC Dallas has been one of the league's best teams at identifying and developing local talent. In 2019 defender Reggie Cannon and midfielder Paxton Pomykal each appeared in at least 25 matches for the Toros. Both were US-born, raised in Texas, and yet to turn 21. Cannon then took the next step in his progression in 2020, when FC Dallas sold him to Portuguese team Boavista.

CHAPTER 4

LONE STAR MOMENTS

When MLS began in 1996, the teams competed for more than the MLS Cup. They also took part in the US Open Cup. Although not as prestigious as the MLS Cup, the US Open Cup had been around since 1913.

The Burn made a deep run in the 1997 US Open Cup. At the time, MLS teams joined the tournament in the third round after lower-level clubs had faced off for two rounds. Dallas started out against the New Orleans Riverboat Gamblers. New Orleans competed in the United Soccer League (USL) A League. After defeating New Orleans 3–0, Dallas moved on to face the Chicago Stingers in the quarterfinals. The Stingers played in the USL's second division. The Burn won that matchup 4–1.

Damián Álvarez (11) scored a big goal for the Burn in the 1997 US Open Cup.

STARS
BURN
11
11

Mark Dodd played a key role as the Burn won their first trophy.

The New York/New Jersey MetroStars awaited in the semifinals. Playing at Baker Field in New York would be a challenge. Plus, the MetroStars had US national team hero Tony Meola in the net. Dallas was equal to the task, however. The Burn took an early lead off the right foot of Damián Álvarez. That one goal was nearly enough. But the MetroStars tied it in the 85th minute.

In extra time, a MetroStars cross went wide and Dallas quickly countered. Defender Wade Webber crossed the ball from the right, and midfielder Jorge Flores was there to finish. Flores volleyed the pass into the net in the 103rd minute. The goal sent Dallas to the 1997 US Open Cup final.

The Burn would meet another familiar opponent, that year's MLS Cup champion DC United, in the final. This time the clubs played 120 minutes without a goal, meaning the game would be decided by penalty kicks. Burn keeper Mark Dodd made a sprawling stop on United's Raúl Díaz Arce—the league's second-leading scorer—in the second round. Meanwhile, Dallas converted its first four attempts. That left the championship on the foot of defender Jorge Rodríguez. The 26-year-old from El Salvador fired a shot low and to the left. And when it found the back of the net, it touched off a wild celebration, as the Burn had their first trophy.

CHASING THE CUP

FC Dallas came into the 2010 season after having missed the playoffs the season before. The season did not start out like the team would have hoped, however. The Toros posted four ties and one loss in its first five games. But the team turned it on midway through the season, setting records in the process.

The Toros won six straight home matches, a feat they'd never accomplished. FC Dallas also set the MLS record for the longest unbeaten road streak at 11 games. The team capped off its memorable 2010 season by setting the MLS record for longest unbeaten streak at 19 games.

The Toros were in position for a deep playoff run. They'd shown they could win wherever they played. That type of resolve proved to be valuable early in the playoffs. FC Dallas hosted Real Salt Lake in the first leg of the conference semifinals. And just five minutes into the match, the Toros trailed 1–0. But as they had done the

El Matador is the Toros' oldest supporters' group.

entire season, the Toros showed fight. Their tough, aggressive defense kept the deficit at one.

With the match still in striking distance, Jeff Cunningham tied the score just before halftime. Cunningham's goal injected life into the Toros and their home crowd. In the second half, a red card on each side made it 10-on-10 soccer for the final 15-plus minutes. With extra time looming, Dallas midfielder Eric Avila scored the go-ahead goal. Avila had just entered the game as a sub a minute earlier. His second goal of the season in the 88th minute gave the Toros a 2–1 victory.

SURVIVE AND ADVANCE

A 1–1 draw in Salt Lake City one week later allowed the Toros to advance by aggregate. The rest of the playoffs would be knockout games. The Toros moved on to face the mighty LA Galaxy in the conference finals. Dallas was a heavy underdog against the star-studded Galaxy, who hosted the match as the top seed in the West.

The Toros showed that this underdog could bite. They took the Galaxy apart in front of their home crowd. With goals from David Ferreira, George John, and Marvin Chávez, the Toros were in total control of the match. The 3–0 defeat was one of the worst ever at home for the Galaxy. The impressive outing also clinched FC Dallas's first MLS Cup appearance.

FC Dallas faced the Colorado Rapids at Toronto's BMO Field in the 2010 MLS Cup. The teams had played to two draws during the regular season. The championship match followed

Eric Avila (12) jumps into the crowd to celebrate his game-winning goal against Real Salt Lake in the 2010 playoffs.

a similar path. Ferreira gave the Toros the lead in the 35th minute. But Conor Casey found the net for Colorado in the 57th minute to tie the score.

The match entered extra time tied 1–1. Then disaster struck for the Toros in the 107th minute. A Rapids player along the end line chipped a crossing pass in front of the Dallas goal. Toros defender John tried to block it with his upper leg, but the ball instead deflected sideways into the net. The own goal

Cristian Colmán scores the first goal in the Toros' 4–0 defeat of Árabe Unido.

held up, and the Colorado Rapids were the 2010 MLS Cup champions, not FC Dallas.

GETTING INTERNATIONAL

The Toros got a taste of international play in the 2016–17 Concacaf Champions League. That's a tournament contested by the top club teams in North America, Central America, and the Caribbean. FC Dallas qualified for the league by posting the top record in the Western Conference in 2015.

During the group stage, FC Dallas earned eight points. This moved the Toros on to the knockout stage, which is played in two legs. The winner would move on to the next round by aggregate. FC Dallas faced Panamanian club Árabe Unido in the quarterfinals. Leg one was played at Toyota Stadium in front of FC Dallas's fans. The Toros struck first and never looked back. Forward Cristian Colmán scored in the 30th minute. Midfielder Kellyn Acosta then scored twice as the Toros cruised to a 4–0 win. They lost the second leg in Panama City but still advanced by aggregate.

Though Dallas lost in the semifinals, the result was not trivial. Only three MLS teams have fared better in the Concacaf Champions League than FC Dallas did that season. It wasn't the league championship that Toros fans have been craving. But it was a strong showing for a club that's still looking to win the big one.

TIMELINE

1995	1996	1997	2004	2005

1995

The Dallas Burn are announced as one of the original 10 MLS teams on June 6.

1996

The Burn play their first MLS game on April 14 against the San Jose Clash.

1997

On October 29 the Burn win their first US Open Cup title in a penalty kick shootout against

2004

Following the season, the Burn change their name to FC Dallas.

2005

FC Dallas plays its first regular-season game at its new stadium in Frisco, Texas, on August 6

TEAM FACTS

FIRST SEASON

1996

STADIUMS

Cotton Bowl (1996–2002, 2004–05)
Dragon Stadium (2003)
Toyota Stadium (2005–)

US OPEN CUP TITLES

1997, 2016

MLS SUPPORTERS' SHIELD

2016

KEY PLAYERS

Michael Barrios (2015–20)
Reggie Cannon (2017–20)
Fabian Castillo (2011–16)
Kenny Cooper (2006–09, 2013)
Jeff Cunningham (2008–10)
Ariel Graziani (1999–2001)
Jason Kreis (1996–2004)
Blas Perez (2012–15)
Paxton Pomykal (2017–)
Carlos Ruíz (2005–2007, 2016)
Maxi Urruti (2016–18)
Dante Washington (1996–99)

KEY COACHES

Dave Dir (1996–2000)
Schellas Hyndman (2008–13)
Óscar Pareja (2014–18)

MLS MOST VALUABLE PLAYER

David Ferreira (2010)
Jason Kreis (1999)

MLS DEFENDER OF THE YEAR

Matt Hedges (2016)

**MLS GOALKEEPER OF
THE YEAR**

Mark Dodd (1996)

**MLS HUMANITARIAN OF
THE YEAR**

Ryan Hollingshead (2017)
Chris Seitz (2012)

MLS ROOKIE OF THE YEAR

Tesho Akindele (2014)

**MLS COMEBACK PLAYER OF
THE YEAR**

Kenny Cooper (2008)
Richard Mulrooney (2006)

MLS COACH OF THE YEAR

Schellas Hyndman (2010)
Óscar Pareja (2016)

GLOSSARY

aggregate
The combined score of both games in a two-game series.

bicycle kick
An acrobatic strike involving a player kicking an airborne ball over his or her head back toward the goal.

campaign
A season.

draw
A game that ends in a tie.

group stage
The part of a tournament when teams are divided into smaller groups or pools; each team faces the others in its group, and those with the best records move on to the knockout stage.

knockout stage
A single-elimination round of a tournament in which one loss eliminates a team.

soccer-specific stadium
A venue built primarily for soccer matches.

striker
A player whose primary responsibility is to create scoring chances and score goals.

supporters' groups
Fan groups that stand and support their team throughout the game by singing, chanting, drumming, waving flags, and more.

winger
An attacking midfielder who plays wide.

MORE INFORMATION

BOOKS

Kortemeier, Todd. *Total Soccer*. Minneapolis, MN: Abdo Publishing, 2017.

Marthaler, Jon. *Ultimate Soccer Road Trip*. Minneapolis, MN: Abdo Publishing, 2019.

Trusdell, Brian. *Soccer Record Breakers*. Minneapolis, MN: Abdo Publishing, 2016.

ONLINE RESOURCES

To learn more about FC Dallas, please visit **abdobooklinks.com** or scan this QR code. These links are routinely monitored and updated to provide the most current information available.

INDEX

ABOUT THE AUTHOR

Sam Moussavi is a novelist and freelance writer based in the San Francisco Bay Area. He has written two sets of young adult novels as well as many nonfiction sports titles.